TaiLorMade Books Presents

UnLawful Vows

By Nataisha T. Hill

May not be suitable for children under the age of 16

Prologue

"One less filth in the world," Sandra mumbled as she trembled so hard that it seemed the four walls of the basement were spinning around her. *Or were they*? She couldn't tell. She could only tell of the tremor inside of her. Her heart rocked in her chest, as though she'd been in a death race. She was visibly shaking. If she grasped an object, it would slither from her grasp and crash down into the floor. She was that unsettled.

Her hair, honey brown and wavy, was drenched with the sweat dripping down her caramel skin. If she wasn't stark naked, her clothes would be just as wet as her hair. It had been days since she last felt the comfort of clothes. At least proper ones. Lately, she was forced to go on without clothes, and when 'they' did let her get dressed, they only provided her with clothes that fuelled their sexual perversion. Vulnerability to the harshness of the extreme weather was nothing new to Sandra at this point.

It didn't matter that she'd been forced to forgo her skincare regimen for many weeks at a stretch. Her skin still looked radiant, holding its rich caramel glow. She was the true definition of a diamond in the rough.

Her knees buckled, seeking to give way as she stood on her feet. As if that wasn't enough to drive her back to the floor, there was the painful throbbing between her legs, where the man, her so-called master, had delivered a blow with his clenched fist. Now he lay nude and motionless, his life sucked out of him. His eyes were wide open, yet seeing nothing.

They were the same eyes that had always been brimming with lust and power when he took her, tossing her back and forth like a ragged doll. It was ironic how she'd strangled him with the very same handcuffs he'd restrained her with. *Poor thing*, she thought and smirked. He definitely hadn't seen it coming. If he'd known the chains of the handcuffs would bring him to his death, he certainly would not have introduced the handcuffs into his perverted game two weeks ago.

Sandra waited for the perfect time to strike. She waited for a moment when he approached her alone, with his wife nowhere in sight. Glancing at the dead man, her eyes were frantic to find the key to the handcuffs. Sandra had found it resting on his chest where it doubled as a pendant. She crouched beside him, yanked the key off his neck and unlocked the cuffs. The cuffs fell to the floor, clanking loudly. She bristled. That was way louder than it should be. She could only hope her boss's wife hadn't heard it.

Careful not to make a sound, she advanced toward the exit, but her plan to be silent was defeated when she mounted the stairs leading out of the basement. The wooden stairs, old and rickety, creaked with each step she took. Without the death sting of iron around her wrists, her skin could finally breathe again. *Freedom, Sandra. That's the smell of freedom.*

Sandra breathed deeply, filling her lungs with fresh air. This air was different. It was poles apart from the stuffed air trapped in the basement, or dungeon as she liked to call it. The air in the basement was rather foul, clogged with the smell of rust, sweat and of course…sex—if sex had a smell.

Sandra had no idea what time it was or what day it was. She'd lost track of time. She barely even knew when it was morning or evening, unless her boss approached her with a derogatory greeting on his cigarette-darkened lips.

The house was quiet, as though there was no sign of life. But she had a feeling her mistress was up there in the master's bedroom. She proceeded toward the stairs leading to the bedroom. Cold sweat dripped down her hair and trailed down her spine, until it found her butt crack. The air conditioner had her perspiration drying up in no time though. Her steps were unhurried, almost soundless, as she made her way to the master's bedroom.

She pushed open the door, her eyes straining to see through the darkness of the room. Her eyes adjusted to the darkness—it was nighttime, obviously—and then her gaze settled on a bump on one side of the bed. Sandra smiled. There Marie was, having her beauty sleep.

She lay on her side, her head resting on one of the many soft pillows on the bed. She'd definitely fallen asleep with the thought that her husband was down there in the basement having his way with their sex slave. Sandra edged closer to Marie and then she halted, her eyes devouring the woman.

She had no idea of killing this one. Marie looked…innocent. Naïve even. What if just like Sandra, Marie had also been sexually enslaved to the pervert? What if their marriage was one huge lie and she also needed saving? More questions crowded Sandra's mind, and then she sat beside Marie and touched her arm through the covers under which she lay.

"Mmmh," Marie hummed, adjusting herself on the bed. "Go shower, Carl. You must stink after being in that pathetic place for hours."

Hours? Sandra wondered. This woman was clearly exaggerating. *Was she drugged?* Perhaps she was too far gone in her slumber to think right. Her husband had only been there for a few minutes. Twenty at the most. He clearly had something even more sinister going on outside of them both, but whatever. None of that mattered at the moment.

Marie was silent again. She had obviously drifted back into sleep. Sandra concluded that she'd been right to think that Marie was naïve. Couldn't she feel that her husband was gone? Couldn't she feel that the person beside her wasn't her Carl? Seriously though, couldn't she feel that something had happened to him? Wasn't there a way these people felt these things? Unless of course, the movies and books were all lying. If this was a movie, she'd definitely feel that her husband was gone. Maybe she'd suddenly feel dizzy, or feel a sharp sting or a stab in her chest. Anything.

This woman felt nothing. She lay there without a care in the world, her chest rising and falling gently as she breathed. Sandra couldn't deny that while she hated every moment with Carl, she'd always looked forward to having sex with Marie. In those few months she was locked up in the dungeon, she realized a truth about herself—one she wished she'd known sooner.

She had a soft spot for women. There was a hole in her life that could only be filled by a woman, and Marie looked perfect.

So, she bent toward Marie and kissed her ear. She ran her hand up and down Marie's arm, and then she whispered, "Come with me. Let us leave this place."

Chapter One

Andrea smiled, her groggy eyes narrowing as a nose-tingling aroma made its way through her lungs. Sonny had made breakfast. Andrea could tell from the aroma that it was a heavenly meal. The man was a great cook, undeniably. He was even a better cook than she was. There was no challenging it. She could only wonder how great a cook his mother had been, since he'd learned everything from her. Sonny had the traits of an absolute workaholic, yet he always made out time to flaunt his cooking skills. *Show off.* That he was. But an outrageously handsome one.

"Rise and shine, beautiful," he said.

Her smile broadened. His sweet voice was the best way to start her morning. It was like a hundred violins playing in harmony.

"Good morning, handsome," she greeted as he stepped into her line of sight.

His face held a glow similar to hers, thanks to the soft smile stretching his beautiful pink lips. He was holding a foldable breakfast tray. The aroma wafting from the kitchen became stronger as he approached, causing Andrea's stomach to clench with a desire to be filled. He placed the tray on the nightstand beside him and then he sat beside her on the bed. Now, his face flooded her vision. She stared into his beautiful brown eyes—the eyes that had entranced her when she first saw them six months ago. It didn't matter that she'd lost count of how many times she got lost in his eyes—they still entranced her no less.

"Morning, beautiful," he stated, returning her greeting.

He lowered his head for what would be a kiss. She smiled, quickly turning her head sideways. She hoped that he wouldn't take offense to it.

"Morning breath," she quickly added.

"Nonsense." He replied and grinned.

She could tell from his voice that his cheeks, just like hers, were inflated with a smile. With her face turned sideways, he planted a kiss on her neck instead.

His lips stayed glued to her neck for a few toe-curling moments, and then he whispered, "Made you breakfast."

"Mmmh," she hummed, smacking her lips together.

When he detached his lips from her skin, she turned toward the tray, but he suddenly caught her lips between his. She chuckled, breaking the kiss, and then she raised herself so that she was slouching against the headboard of the bed. Sonny turned sideways to fetch the tray, and then he placed it on the bed. He'd made breakfast burritos.

"Oh my gosh, Sonny!" she exclaimed. "Thank you so much."

"For pampering you?" he asked. "If I don't, who will?"

He wiggled his brows at her. Her heart throbbed in response. *Gosh, he's so sexy. I can't believe he's mine.* His brows were so full, yet in shape. They formed beautiful arcs on his hazel eyes. That on his spotless caramel brown skin was sheer perfection. It was no wonder she always got lost in his eyes. It mesmerized her how a man could be so perfect without even trying.

His hair was dark and glossy. It was a little overgrown for a low-cut, but the heavy curls it retained were to die for. Andrea could do nothing but smile the whole time that he fed her.

"You deserve to be treated like a queen," he said. "You worked so hard last night."

He smiled no doubt because he was exaggerating. The previous night, they'd moved into their new home in an upscale neighborhood. But there'd been nothing hectic about the move because they'd hired a moving company to handle the whole process. Andrea had barely lifted a thing. The only thing she'd done was treat Sonny to a sensual massage. Her breath slowed as images from the previous night crowded her reasoning.

Andrea had skin of olive, contrasting with his honey golden skin. But that was where the whole beauty lay—in the contrast. There had not been better way to spend their first night together in their new home, and their twelfth day together as newlyweds.

"…you always work hard." He continued, feeding her another spoon.

"Not as hard as you," she said.

Sonny owned a technical computer servicing company where he made a six figure income monthly. So, if there was anyone who worked super hard, it was he. It was in fact one of the things she adored about him. That, and his sweet personality, had drawn her to him like ants to sugar.

As she thought about his job, her gaze suddenly rested on his white shirt. "Oh my gosh! What time is it?"

Her curious eyes found the clock on the wall. It took a while for her to focus in on the hour hand since the beams from the sun seeped through the blinds. It was a few minutes past seven in the morning.

"Sonny!" she gasped. "You should get going! You're gonna be late for work!"

"Chill, love," he said. "It's not like I'm gonna get fired or anything. I just wanna spend time with you is all..."

"I also want to spend time with you, love." She said, transferring the tray to the other side of the bed and out of his reach. "But we can do that when you're back from work. And besides, I wouldn't wanna mess up your beautiful white shirt...or crumple it..."

"And if I want you to?" He leaned in toward her and kissed her before she could say a word.

This time, he didn't give her a chance to remind him of her morning breath. In no time, his body was crushing hers, slowly lowering her to the bed until her back was almost flat against it.

"Know what? Fuck that office. I wanna spend my day with my beautiful wife." He started to undo the buttons of his shirt.

"Sonny, the tray," she reminded.

He rose from the bed and moved the tray to the nightstand, and then he returned to Andrea. His eyes burned into hers, and then he lowered his gaze to the rest of her body. She was dressed in a sleeveless silk nightgown, yet his gaze instantly warmed her skin. He unbuttoned his shirt. His pace was slow and calm. She wondered how a man could be so relaxed while his stare caused her to unnerve.

Her heart was beating twice as loud while her entire body had given into the surge of adrenaline. She could already feel warmth pooling at the depth of her stomach. His eyes undressed her, stripping off her gown before his hands even got to do so. She lay there in bed, watching him with a heaving chest. Her breath was growing raspy as wave after wave of adrenaline flowed through her.

Sonny tossed his shirt aside and then he rid himself of his pants right after. At five foot eight, he was just as tall as she was. Maybe only taller by an inch or two. Then again, she wasn't so crazy about the numbers. Besides, she found it more romantic that she could stare into her husband's eyes and kiss him without needing to stand on her tippy toes or tilt her head noticeably. Somehow, it made her feel closer to him.

Her eyes roamed his body as he approached her. She could not say that he had a ripped midsection, but he wasn't chubby either. He was just perfect—her definition of sexy. That was the one word she found most appropriate to describe him with. Her bone-straight, dark-root brown hair was now a mess. It was scattered around her head, tickling her neck as she lay there on the bed. But she was too lost in Sonny to move a muscle.

"I could stare at you all day," he said, staring at her in a way that made her feel flawless, as though she didn't have a litter of freckles on her face.

Unfortunately, he didn't have all day. The doorbell chimed in, bringing an abrupt end to their romantic moment.

"Perfect timing!" Sonny rolled his eyes.

The gesture was almost feminine. It made Andrea laugh. "I'll get it," she said.

Andrea had known the neighbors would likely come say hello to them. She just hadn't expected it to be so early. She rose from the bed and proceeded toward the door.

"Uhm..." Sonny began, clearing his throat. "I think you're forgetting something."

She turned toward him and wasn't surprised to find him holding her jacket. She smirked. "Jealous much?"

"Just for the cold," he said.

She could tell it was a little white lie, but there was a sliver of cold, so she could really use the jacket. His hands brushed her skin as he helped her into it. His hands left tingles all over her skin, making her crave more of his touch. She breathed deeply, her body aching for him in a way she'd never ached for another man.

Sonny was unlike any other man she'd encountered. Besides him being the only interracial man that she'd ever dated, there was something about him that drew her ever nearer, ever closer. He had a level of understanding that no other man could compare. That was what made her tick. If she didn't know better she'd say he'd gone somewhere for an intensive training on how to treat a woman right. *Such a heartthrob.*

"The door," Sonny's voice cut through her thoughts.

"Oh." She snapped out of her trance and headed downstairs.

Once she arrived at the door, Andrea looked through the peephole. A blonde was standing right in front, with her back to the door. Just before Andrea opened it, she took a moment to tie the belt of her robe. The blonde turned around with a smile on her face. She was apparently a few years older than Andrea. She was probably in her late twenties, just like Sonny.

"Hey!" The blonde greeted with her smile ever-so-present.

She had a bubbly personality—it was as evident as the fullness of the rack on her chest. Andrea had only just met her but she reminded her of her very lively best friend in high school.

"Hey," Andrea greeted back, flashing the woman a smile, but the smile was nowhere as excited as the woman's.

"I'm Heather!" the woman said. "And you're the new neighbor! I got home pretty late last night and didn't even realize someone new had moved in across from me."

She made her way into the house. Andrea stared at her, stunned that she'd stepped in so casually as though it were her own home. She shook her head, a small smile forming on her lips. The woman really did remind her of her best friend.

Heather froze in her tracks and then she clamped on her lips with her palms as she turned to face Andrea. "Oh my gosh! Where are my manners?"

Andrea chuckled.

"Pardon me," Heather said. "I'm just so freaking excited about having a new neighbor."

"I share your excitement, girl!" Andrea said. "Oh, I'm Andrea by the way."

She presented her right hand for a shake. She was unsure if this was the right thing to do. Maybe a hug would do it better, but she settled for a handshake instead. She gasped when Heather suddenly hugged her. For a moment there, it seemed like they were old time friends who'd just met each other again after forever.

"I'm so excited to meet you!" Heather said.

Although Andrea couldn't completely relate, Heather's excitement was pretty much visible in the tone of her voice. Her voice was high-pitched, close to a squeal. Andrea noticed how Heather's chest crushed hers, oppressing the moderate boobs found there—but in a good way. However, Andrea couldn't shake the fact that there was something eerie about this introduction. She couldn't put her finger on it, but something definitely felt strange.

Chapter Two

Getting along with the neighbor would be so easy. But then, there was the fact that the woman was sparsely dressed, and Andrea wasn't even the least cozy with that. Heather was wearing a red bikini top and denim shorts—very skimpy shorts that bared her thighs just as much as the bikini top bared her chest. Andrea wasn't so concerned about the shorts though—at least not as much as she was about the bikini top. Heather had ample skin on her chest. They were roughly twice Andrea's. Years ago, she would have found this intimidating, but a lot had changed about her since she met Sonny. He loved her the way she was, like she was the only girl in the world. And that was all she needed to change her view of herself.

Heather's top was having a hell of a time containing her twin mounds. It was a rather disturbing sight. Andrea glanced up the stairs. She could only hope Sonny didn't come down anytime soon.

Heather glanced around the house. "Is there anything I can help with? I can help you unpack, put things in order…"

"Oh, no." Andrea said. "Thanks for offering to help though." Heather suddenly grinned. "Who's the lucky man?"

"Wha…" Andrea started to ask, but then she trailed off as she found Heather staring at her left hand.

Heather's eyes were trained on the diamond ring on Andrea's ring finger. The ring held an eye-catching display of interlocking rows of diamonds and sapphires, with a larger piece of diamond mounted at the center.

Andrea blushed, finally getting Heather's question. "My husband is upstairs."

"Oh, I'd love to say hello." Heather's eyes suddenly brightened up as she glanced at the stairway. "Ah! There he is!"

Andrea followed Heather's gaze. She held her breath hoping that Sonny had made himself decent before heading downstairs. She only released her breath when she saw that he was wearing a beige t-shirt and black pants.

"Quite a catch," Heather whispered to Andrea.

Andrea blushed some more. She hadn't thought Sonny had heard Heather, but Sonny's words told her the opposite.

"Heard that," he said with a smile. He stepped into the living room, regarding Heather with a curious yet playful look. "I suppose you are our neighbor."

"Oui!" All smiles, Heather outstretched her right hand for a shake. "Name's Heather! I live just across from you!"

Sonny took her hand. "Sonny." He let go once he uttered his name.

"Well, Sonny, Andrea, it's a pleasure meeting you both." Heather looked from Sonny to Andrea. "My husband would love to meet you too, but he's one hell of a career man, always on business trips."

She smiled, almost wistfully, and then her lips parted to let out some more words, but the frantic howls of a dog was an end to whatever she was going to say. "Oh," she said, "Sandy is awake now. I guess I'll see you guys later."

"Thank you so much for coming over," Andrea said.

"See you around!" Heather waved them goodbye, and then she was gone.

The dog wouldn't stop howling. "Keep it down, Sandy!" The rest of Heather's words were lost in the wind as she stepped further away from the house.

Andrea leaned sideways, resting her head on Sonny's shoulder. "She seems nice."

"Totally!" Sonny said. "Glad you've made a friend, even though you didn't actually make an effort to find one."

"I don't need to." She wrapped her arms around him. "I have you."

"Aww." Sonny lifted her face with both hands and then he planted a soft kiss on her lips. "You know, I was actually thinking of getting you a doggie to keep you company while I was at work."

"This is not up for a debate, Sonny. You're getting me one." She playfully rolled her eyes, and then she suddenly remembered breakfast. "Oh my gosh... I gotta get back to my food."

She'd barely taken a step from Sonny when she heard the doorbell. She turned toward Sonny who'd plopped down on a chair a split-second before they heard the bell.

"Talk about some super caring neighbors," he said, his voice low.

Andrea chuckled as she gave him a playful smack on the head before going to the door. She found a petite woman staring at her with a brilliant smile once she got there. The woman was no less than twenty years older than she was, and the bold strands of gray hair on her head were an indication of that.

"Cookies?" the woman asked, grinning. She was holding a small basket of cookies. She presented it to Andrea, her laugh lines becoming more apparent as her grin broadened.

Andrea welcomed her offer with a smile. "Why, thank you, Mrs —"

"Penelope," the woman said. "Just Penelope."

"Thank you so much, Penelope."

"Call me Penny though. The 'lope' in it makes me feel really old, for some odd reason."

"Oh, Penny it is then."

Penelope handed over the basket. "Hoping you enjoy eating them just as much as I enjoyed making them."

"Oh, I sure will."

"What's your name, love?"

"Andrea."

"Well, Andrea, I'm the cookie granny who lives just over there." Penelope turned around and pointed at an apartment building. "Flat three is where you'll find me."

"I guess I'll be visiting you more often then," Andrea said.

"That would be great." Penelope chuckled. "I actually saw you moving in yesterday. I hope you like it here."

"Oh, believe me I already do. The neighborhood feels so heavenly."

"Careful though." Penelope's smile dropped as the words left her lips. She edged toward Andrea, and when she spoke again, her voice was the tiniest of whispers. "Green snake in the green grass." She added, glancing over her shoulder at Heather's house. She turned back toward Andrea and shook her head.

"Be careful," she said.

"Okay?" Andrea asked, an unsure smile crossing her face.

"...of home wrecking Heather."

Chapter Three

Such a bitch! Andrea thought. Penelope's words had been on Andrea's mind since their first encounter four days ago. There was no reason to doubt her. The woman would gain nothing from tarnishing Heather's image. So, the chances of her lying were as slim as the chances of Heather being a proper woman. Andrea sighed. She couldn't believe how naïve she'd been, letting a stranger walk into her home dressed like that when her husband was there.

The slut was on a home wrecking mission. That was probably why she'd visited. It had to be. Heather probably didn't even want to be friends with her or anything, Andrea slowly realized. She'd only come to check out the man of the house, and of course she liked what she saw. Andrea boiled with rage as memories from four days ago drifted into her head. She could vividly see Heather's face in her mind's eye. She could see her smile—a smile she would gladly knock off her face now—and that damned rack on the woman's chest.

"Gosh, I can't believe how stupid I was."

"Are you okay?" Sonny asked, his face etched with concern.

Andrea had been helping Sonny's feet into his patent oxford shoes, but then she'd slowed down as thoughts of Heather struck her. She actually hadn't realized she'd said those words aloud until Sonny asked if she was okay.

"Of course," she said. "I was just remembering back when I threw away some heels because I couldn't get them laced right."

She looked up at him, flashing him a reassuring smile. She was crouching beside their bed, just in front of Sonny who was watching her the whole time. She was still wearing the sleeveless white night dress she'd slept in, so Sonny was probably having a nice view of her cleavage from where he sat. Scratch that, he definitely was. She could tell from his now drooping eyes that he wanted to hold them and knead them, as typical of him. Her cheeks heated up as she thought of his hands all over her chest, rubbing her breasts.

Sonny was all dressed up for work, his torso enclosed in a formal white shirt, while a pair of dark brown trousers enclosed the lower half of his body. He was the perfect gentleman, his shirt tucked in so decently, giving an undisturbed view of his luxury leather black belt. Done with his shoes, she adjusted the hem of his pants and then she rose to her feet. He stood up as well, an arm encircling her slim waist.

"You sure you're okay?" He asked.

"Yes. I'll just miss you is all."

"Is this you asking me to skip work to be with you again?" He wiggled his brows.

"No! Of course not!" She feigned horror, and then she clapped her hands together. "Okay, okay. It's time to leave now."

She hurried across the room and picked up his car keys from the vintage coffee table. She returned to Sonny to place them in his right hand.

"Time to—" she started, but the doorbell cut her off.
Seriously? She thought. *It was barely even seven!* Andrea rolled her eyes. *I swear if it's that nasty bitch, I'm putting her in her place!*

"Maybe it's the old lady with some more cookies," Sonny said.

Andrea desperately wanted to believe he was right, but he wasn't. It took only a few moments for them to find out. Once they arrived in the living room, Andrea unlocked the main door. Heat flared up inside of her at the sight of Heather. The pathetic bitch was undoubtedly up to no good. She was dressed just as sparsely as she had on their first meeting.

"Hey Andrea," Heather greeted. "Good morning, Sonny," She chimed, waving at them, and although she had an innocent smile on her face, Andrea could see a gleam in her eyes that couldn't be anything but lust.

"Morning, Heather," Sonny said. "Sleep well, yes?"

"Of course," Heather said.

Damn it, Sonny. Please don't encourage her. Andrea thought.

"My car battery is dead though." She pouted. "I was wondering if you could…uhm…give me a hand. If that isn't too much to ask."

Her eyes were fixed on Sonny the whole time.

"I'd be glad to!" Andrea offered.

She feigned oblivion to a drop in Heather's mood, even though the drop was as noticeable as the sag of her breasts. "My husband is already late for work, so let's just let him leave and then…" Andrea leaned toward Heather and whispered in a rather chirpy voice, "…we can have some girl time!"

"Sounds great!" Sonny glanced at his Rolex. "Gotta rush."

He wrapped Andrea in a quick hug. "You take care, beautiful," he said.

When he tried to break the embrace a moment later, Andrea pulled him closer and kissed him. She made sure to let her lips linger on his. That should be enough to tie a knot in Heather's stomach. Andrea turned to look at Heather. The smile on the woman's face had morphed into a grimace. *Take that, bitch!*

"I love you so much Sonny," Andrea said.

"I love you more, babe," Sonny said. He gave Heather a small smile, and then he ducked into the front passenger seat of his black Audi.

Andrea stood beside Heather, her hands crossed over her chest. Heather's arms were folded as well. The two women stood side by side, neither one saying a word to the other. They watched until Sonny's car was out of sight. Andrea suddenly turned toward Heather, yanked her by the arm and glared at her. Heather gasped, her eyes widening.

"Now you listen, Heather Home Wrecking bitch," Andrea said, "I see what you're doing. I know how hard you're trying to get my husband to notice you."

"What?" Heather feigned oblivion. "Why would—"

"I'm not gonna say this again." Andrea clenched her teeth. "Stay away from Sonny! I've been through too many bad relationships to allow a hussy like you to ruin my good life. I am everything to that man. Besides, my husband certainly isn't interested in your saggy boobs!"

"Oh my gosh!" Heather gasped, snatching her arm out of Andrea's hold. "I can't believe that you would say this to me. You don't even know me. You just met me."

Heather's eyes were rounded with horror. If Andrea didn't know better she'd say the woman was truly innocent. But she knew Heather was far from it. Everything about her demeanor had proved it. Andrea smirked, knowing that her words had hit home.

"What?" Andrea asked. "You know you've been practically rubbing that unimpressive pair on his face. But really, saggy boobs don't move him. Sonny is a man of great taste. So darling, you best be of good behavior and know your place. Oh, and—"

Andrea clicked her tongue, her eyes roaming Heather's torso. She shook her head and then she reached out to move a lock of hair behind Heather's head. The misguided lock of hair had been trying to cover her left eye. Andrea didn't want that. She wanted to see the look in the woman's eyes when she spoke to her about her impropriety. She wanted to watch every word sink in.

"…just in case you ever need some proper clothes," Andrea added, "my house is barely a minute away."

With a smug smile stealing its way across her lips, Andrea turned away from the dazzled home wrecker and advanced toward her house. She felt accomplished.

"Someone has been filling your head with lies about me," Heather said. "It was that old hag, wasn't it?"

Andrea turned toward her with a smile. "Nobody had to tell me anything, darling. It's written all over your face."

"You don't know anything about me." Heather insisted.

Andrea's smile stayed plastered to her face as she stared at Heather and waved goodbye. She knew that was enough to tighten Heather's stomach with fury. So when she saw Heather's nose flaring, she knew she was hitting home. Heather didn't say another word. She whirled around on her heels, stormed off into her house and slammed the door behind her.

Over the next couple of weeks, Heather became non-existent to Andrea. There were no more early morning knocks or parading of that woman's body in front of her husband. The few times that they did see Heather was when she was coming to or leaving her residence. Otherwise, Andrea wouldn't have even known that she lived next door. The woman was a snail, retreating into her shell where she stayed hidden.

Chapter Four

Tanya had a baby. Judging from Tanya's outrageously huge baby bump when he last saw her two weeks ago, Sonny had known this day was around the corner. He just hadn't expected it to happen on a day he was so exhausted from work. He knew where this would lead, and he didn't like it one bit. Andrea, however, seemed to be on cloud nine. Scratch that, she WAS on cloud nine. Her face had been glowing with a smile since he stepped into the house, and now as he watched her rummage their mirrored closet for an outfit, he saw her smile broadening some more.

"I'm so excited!" she said. "My sister has always wanted a baby."

Well, don't you all? Sonny stayed silent. He would not speak until he had found the right words to say. What more was there to say? He'd already told Andrea he was happy for Tanya. That was all he needed to say, wasn't it? He'd already agreed to drive Andrea to the hospital to see the baby after all.

"Pink or blue?" Andrea asked, turning to face him.

She was holding a blue dress and a pink dress. They looked pretty much the same, with back zippers, three quarter sleeves and midi lengths.

Sonny shrugged. "Same difference."

He didn't see why she was so worked up about wanting to look good for the baby. He didn't want to come off as cranky, but why look good for some baby who couldn't even see you? Tanya's baby was only a few hours old! He certainly couldn't see a thing. So, any dress would work. It wasn't like she was dressing to impress Tanya or her husband any way. Sonny couldn't be bothered about finding the 'perfect' outfit. He'd settled for a casual blue and white t-shirt and matching jeans.

"I'm actually considering the blue," Andrea said.

"My God, Andrea!" Sonny exclaimed. "You look perfect even without clothes on! It's not like you're going on a date or anything."

"Oh…" Andrea turned back toward the closet. Her mood seemed to drop, but it rose back up barely a moment later. "Blue it is then."

Sonny smiled as Andrea returned the pink dress to the closet. His wife looked perfect in whatever outfit, but he'd secretly hoped she went for the blue dress. The polyester dress was snug and cozy, highlighting every shape and contour of her body in a way that made him want to wrap his arms around her. So, it was impossible to knock an amorous smile off his face as he watched her. With her back to him, she slowly clothed herself in the blue dress, and then she reached backward to fasten the zipper.

This was Sonny's favorite part, so he rose from the armchair where he'd been sitting with his legs crossed at the thighs, and then he crossed the room to meet Andrea. He watched her through the mirror, his eyes zeroing in on her smile as she slowly let go of the zipper and let her hands fall to her sides. He slowly zipped up her dress, his fingers using every split second to tease her skin. Andrea held her breath, her smile suddenly turning sultry as she locked eyes with him. She leaned backward, into his embrace as his arms wrapped around her.

"Thank you," she said in a low voice.

Sonny kissed her shoulder, teasing her bare skin with his soft lips. Off-shoulder dresses meant shoulder kisses. Lots of them.

He looked up at her with a smile. "Ready?"

"Ready when you are, handsome."

The hospital was no less than thirty minutes away from home. The drive, however, would be five to ten minutes shorter if Sonny drove a little faster. But he saw no reason to. What's the rush? Besides, he loved the feel of having his wife beside him in his car. Her legs were crossed at the thighs, and when he glanced up her body, the sight of her stomach filled his heart with warmth. Her stomach was as flat as a model's. She'd been that way since he first met her, and would always stay that way, because there would never be a baby to alter her perfection.

Andrea was staring out through the window the whole time, watching other cars zoom past. Although she was looking away from him, he could tell that she had a lot on her mind. He hoped though, that it wasn't what he was thinking. She was never to think about having a baby. Why give undue attention to things that could never be? Why let the things you could never have steal away your joy?

Andrea was a brave woman. She knew better than to let unwholesome thoughts cloud her mind. Or so Sonny wanted to believe. If it were up to him, he would wind down the windows so he could bask in the chilly night air, but the air would ruffle Andrea's hair, and that wouldn't be pleasant. She'd spent a slice of her time in front of the mirror, brushing every strand into place and perfecting her edges. Messing it all up was the last thing he wanted.

Her face was blank, devoid of a smile. Sonny would give anything to fix that. He reached sideways, his palm finding her left thigh. She glanced down at her thigh, and then up at him.

"You look beautiful, darling," he said.

She smiled. "For you."

Sonny grinned as he pulled into the premises of the hospital. There now, that was the Andrea he knew—the beautiful woman with a radiant smile. Soon after he parked the car, they were standing side by side in an elevator headed for the third floor of the four-story building. The door chimed open when they reached the third floor, and as they made their way out of the rather crowded enclosure, Sonny stuck his hands into the front pockets of his pants. He walked beside Andrea, his footsteps not half as bold as hers. Well, that was because her feet were shod in a pair of chunky heeled sandals while he'd gone for an almost soundless pair of sneakers. He stepped in after Andrea as she let herself into room 45.

"Tanya!" she squealed, hastening toward her sister who lay in bed, dressed in a blue johnny. "Oh my gosh! Congratulations, girl."

She sat beside Tanya, and then she wrapped her in an embrace. "Congratulations, girl!" she echoed.

Tanya grinned. "Thank you. I actually didn't think you'd come tonight. It's pretty late."

"I couldn't go to bed without meeting my new nephew!" Andrea said. "I finally have a nephew!"

Sonny glanced sideways, at a crib where a tiny child lay sound asleep. He swallowed a lump in his throat, and then he looked back at the sisters. Tanya was staring right at him.

He had only two words on his lips. "Congratulations, Tanya."

Chapter Five

Andrea and Sonny crashed their way through their living room, their lips locked together. The house was unlit; the only source of light was the moonlight streaking in through a crack between the curtains. That was enough to give Andrea an outline of the house. She led Sonny toward the bedroom, her hands frantically ripping off his clothes. It took a moment for her to rid him of his shirt.

His hands were just as frantic. While he pulled her closer with his left hand, his right hand found her zipper and yanked it down. Andrea shrugged out of her dress, her lips momentarily leaving his. But once the dress was out of the way, she found his lips again. She kissed him hard and deep, her whole body trembling with need. Sonny exhaled deeply—it was a sound that could pass for a moan.

He shoved her into a wall, his hands roaming her now unclothed body. Andrea's back was flat against the wall. Her legs started to go weak as Sonny deepened the kiss. She tilted her head backward, momentarily breaking the kiss for a breather. She flattened her left palm to the wall, groping for the light switch. But when his lips found her neck, all thoughts of finding the switch were forgotten. She moaned, her breath hot and raspy. She dug her fingers into his hair and grabbed fistfuls of it.

Eager to feel the rest of his body, her hands glided down the back of his neck, and then they started to roam his shoulders. Sonny's shoulders were rather narrow, as opposed to the broad shoulders most men had. But it suited him just fine.

Andrea gasped when the lights suddenly turned on, and then she glanced sideways to find Sonny's hand on the switch. A smile broke out on her face just before he scooped her into his arms and led her toward the bed. She wrapped an arm around his neck and lifted her head for another kiss. He obliged, his lips kneading hers until he settled her on her side of the bed. She shut her eyes, keeping every image out of sight.

"You're so beautiful, Andrea," he whispered into her left ear. His breath against her skin caused her to tremble. She could feel her skin tingling as goose bumps erupted all over it. "...so beautiful I can't believe you're mine." He added, kissing her again, this time, going for her neck.

She rocked her head back, a moan escaping her slightly parted lips. She waited for another kiss, but then she felt him pull away. He undid his zipper and got rid of his pants, and then he leaned toward her again, poking her with his hardness. She gasped, her mouth going dry with need.

"The condoms," he whispered, "...are there any left?"

Her eyes narrowing open, she nodded. "Yes…" Once she felt him move, she grabbed his arm and yanked him back down.

"Just a second," he said.

"Please, Sonny." She stared into his eyes. "Please…I want to feel you. Skin to skin. Just this once…"

Sonny clamped his lips together. He seemed to be deep in thoughts. Whatever he was thinking, Andrea hoped he finally agreed with her. It had been so long since she felt his raw skin against hers. She needed that—the adrenaline that could only come from the unprotected contact. She wanted to feel him, with no rubber coming in the way of her pleasure.

"Please." Her eyes pleaded, melting into his.

She arched her back and slowly peeled off her panties. She kicked off the flimsy fabric, and then she grabbed his left hand. Her eyes stayed fixed on his as she led his hand between her legs. She slowly brushed it along her wet snatch. "Feel that? I am so wet. For you. No rubber, Sonny. Please…"

Sonny grunted. Finally deciding, he moved her hand out of the way, and then he positioned himself at her entrance, his body nudging her legs apart.

Oh, gosh, yes! Andrea bit her lower lip to suppress a moan. It was a few minutes past midnight, and the night was as quiet as it could ever be. She feared that if she dared become vocal, her voice would slice through the silence, so she kept it all bottled up.

She squirmed beneath him as he stuffed her with his girth. He started to thrust, slow and deep. His hands traced the sides of her body, mounting the curves of her waist until they disappeared behind her back to undo her bra straps. With her bra now out of the way, he lowered his head and took a nipple in his mouth. His lips were warm around her skin, giving her a moist massage as he sucked ever so gently. He cupped her untouched breast with his right hand and started to massage it, giving it just as much attention as he gave the other.

He kept up with his thrusts. They were slow and deep. She was dripping wet between her legs—the perfect lube. Her warm juices spread around his manhood, making it glide effortlessly in and out of her. Her chest heaved as her heart started to pace. She squealed with delight, clenching around Sonny and giving it a gentle squeeze. Sonny moaned as he switched to her other nipple. His stomach was flat against hers, their bodies molded together without a sliver of space. She'd thought he was the deepest he could get, but when he suddenly pushed deeper, stabbing his way toward her cervix, she let out a soft cry, her fingers roaming his back until they found the perfect spot to dig into.

She wrapped her legs around him, keeping him buried inside of her as he pounded her. And even when her legs started to tremble, she held them in place. Each thrust shoved her toward her climax. She needed him inside of her when she came. He grunted, his lips crawling through her cleavage until they met hers. He locked lips with her, but he broke the kiss almost immediately, and then he whispered four words into her ear.

"I love you, Andrea."

"I love you too, Sonny," she said in between whimpers as Sonny kept hammering her.

He had picked up pace. She could feel a sense of urgency in his new rhythm. The sheets crumpled beneath them, and she arched her back, thrusting up to meet him. She grinded into him while orbiting herself around his shaft.

"Oh, Andrea!" he moaned. "Keep this up and you'll make me cum inside of you."

"What if I wanted you to?" she asked.

Sonny bristled. He propped himself up on his elbows and stared into her face. "Do you?" he asked, his cold voice causing her to flinch.

She could only stare back at him. No words could make it through the tightness of her throat. She hoped though, that he could see right through her and grasp her deepest desires. Sonny had always given her all that she wanted, never minding the cost. He'd always pampered her, going to great lengths just to make her happy. Why couldn't he just see that seeding her womb was the one true way to make her happy?

"Wait a minute," Sonny suddenly pulled out of her.

A rush of air stole its way inside of her but she barely had a moment to dwell on the emptiness overwhelming her. Her eyes were fixated on Sonny as he knitted his brows together in concentration. The affectionate look in his eyes had melted away, replaced with a wariness that made her stomach unsettle.

"You had this planned all along, didn't you?" he asked. "That's why you didn't let me use protection. You want me to get you pregnant, Andrea."

Andrea's throat tightened even more as she struggled to fight back her tears.

He sprang to his feet. "Do you even take those fucking pills?"

Andrea shuddered. Sonny had never raised his voice at her. For the first time, she saw his eyes grow cold, his flaring nose evident of the surge of adrenaline inside of him.

"Please, calm down," she said.

She rose from the bed and approached him. He didn't say a word. He just stood there unmoving. She halted in front of him, and then she touched his arm. Her touch was light as a feather. She waited for a reaction, and when it didn't come, she held him with her two hands.

"Sonny." She stared into his eyes. "I love you so much. So much that I want to…"

She lowered her head and led his hand to her stomach. She flattened his palm to her bare skin, right where her womb should be, and then she looked up at him with a smile. A lone tear strolled out of her left eye, dampening her cheek.

"I want to feel a part of you inside of me," she said.

Sonny shook his head. "We had a deal, Andrea. You are not to speak of this. Ever." He snatched back his arm.

"Sonny—"

"Enough, woman! We are never making babies. The sooner you accept it, the better." He grabbed his pants and a pillow, and then he stormed out of the room, slamming the door behind him.

Tears streaked down Andrea's cheeks. She stared at the door, her feet rooted to the same spot she'd been standing a minute ago. She'd go after him, but it didn't strike her as a great idea. Letting him cool off seemed like the right thing to do. There was no way she could approach him in that mood. It would only upset him even more and that was the last thing she wanted. She had never seen him so infuriated. She had no idea what he would do to her if she dared approach him after he'd left for some time alone.

It was at that moment she realized she didn't know her husband the way she'd thought she did. She'd been so sure he wouldn't react so hurtfully. She'd been so sure he'd handle this like an adult that he was. But he hadn't. It made her wonder what else she didn't know about Sonny. They'd been married for two and a half years. *Shouldn't that be enough time to know all there was to know about him*? She'd waited two whole years to bring up her desire to have a child because she'd thought the passage of time would weaken his resolve to not have a child. Turned out she was wrong.

Chapter Six

She wondered what else she was wrong about. Who really was he? Somehow, she felt like he was hiding something. It was more than just a hunch. It was a feeling that had been seeking to overwhelm her since the past year, but she'd never given it any thought because she'd been certain that their six months of courtship had been a perfect foundation.

But there were things that didn't add up. She'd never met his family. Hell, he didn't even have any friends. Sure, he'd told her his parents were dead and he had no siblings. Yet, she felt he wasn't telling her the whole truth. During their courtship she'd been too drunk in love to think much about it. And now that she did, she didn't like the flicker of fear burning inside of her. This would be a lot easier if he was from the United States. But no, he was Australian, so it would be difficult—no, impossible was the right word—to locate any of his friends or schools.

"Damn it!" She muttered. "There has to be a way."

All she knew about the man was his name, Sonny Adams, his job as a successful business owner, and then his nationality. It now bothered her that she knew nothing else about the man she'd married. Unless she counted the fact that she knew his age—if he actually was twenty-nine as he claimed.

When she had met Tanya's baby for the first time, there had been a sudden change inside of her. Meeting him had awakened her desire to be a mother, to have a child of her own, cradled in her arms. When she had looked up at Sonny she thought he felt it too. She thought she saw the same desire in his eyes. So, she'd concluded there would never be a time more perfect to bring up the conversation.

Andrea sighed, jolting out of her thoughts. She walked over to the closet and retrieved her night robe, and after she'd thrown it on, she walked over to her phone which sat idly on the dressing mirror vanity unit. She hadn't taken her phone along with her to the hospital because she hadn't seen a need to. She barely received any phone calls. Andrea had an idea that may resolve her curiosity.

She picked up her phone and browsed through her contact list. Sonny would never forgive her if he found out that she was going to pay to get his social security number investigated, but this was a risk that she was willing to take. If all else failed, her sister's friend, Olivia worked for a diagnostic laboratory. Andrea was determined by any means to get whatever information that she could find.

A few days later at the office, Olivia slowly opened the top drawer of the white table in front of her. She dragged her fingertips across a large envelope in the drawer, and then she sighed. Delivering bad news was not one of her strengths. But this was something she had to do. When Andrea had suddenly showed up at the DNA lab with a sample of her husband's blood, Olivia had been appalled that Andrea was trying to investigate her husband. Why would she even think of that?

This was not something Olivia enjoyed doing, but she could not say no to her friend's only sister. Whatever Andrea's reasons were, they had to be good. Andrea had only come running to her after her attempt to investigate his social security number had failed. There had to be a reason a woman would go to such lengths.

And now, with the results in her hands, Olivia was only glad she had agreed to help. She just needed to find a way to break the news. Then again, did she even need to? All she had to do was hand over the envelope. She shut the drawer and fetched her phone from the left pocket of her lab coat. She took a deep breath, her beady eyes blinking behind geeky spectacles.

"You have to do this, Olivia," she muttered. "Andrea has to know."

She plopped down on a stool and called Andrea's cell phone. It went straight to voicemail, so Andrea had left instructions to call her land line. It was answered after two rings, but no one said a word.

"Hey Andrea," Olivia finally said.

"Hey."

"Are you okay?" Olivia asked.

"Uhm...yeah, I—" a sneeze cut off the conversation. "Just a little cold is all."

"Oh," Olivia said. "I'm so sorry about that. I hope you get better soon."

"Thank you." A momentary silence passed between them. "What's up?"

Olivia breathed deeply. "I'm afraid I have some horrific news about your husband."

"You have news about my husband?"

"Well, yeah. You know that information that you asked me about? Well, I found something out."

"Oh my goodness! How bad is it?"

"I really can't give you details over the phone. We should meet up tonight, after work."

"Okay..."

Olivia couldn't ignore the fact that Andrea's voice had dropped to a whisper. She knew Andrea had said that she was sick, but she sounded more awful as she spoke. Olivia could still pick out the brittleness in it as she talked.

"How bad is it, Olivia? I can't be left in suspense."

"I'm afraid he is a she," Olivia broke the news.

"Shit! No way!"

"I'll be done with work in the next eight hours. So, let's meet outside my workplace by 10p.m. I'll be waiting at the alleyway."

"Okay..."

"Andrea?"

"Yeah?"

"Whatever you do, you can't let your husband find out. At this point, I'm not sure what he or she is capable of."

Olivia wanted to believe it was the cold, but a voice in her head told her that the sound she'd heard was Andrea's quiet sobbing. *Wouldn't she want to see the evidence first?* Then again, news like this would likely make anyone cry. Before Olivia could utter another word, the line went dead.

Chapter Seven

Andrea advanced toward Sonny. She could only hope that he wasn't still angry. Besides, she didn't want him to suspect anything regarding what she was up to. She was hoping that Olivia would reach out to her soon regarding any information that she had found. Until then, she knew that she had to play nice.

Sonny was seated in the Jacuzzi, his head bent downward as he scrubbed his thighs with a bath puff. He must have heard her footsteps, because he suddenly raised his head, his eyes finding hers right away.

"Good morning, Sonny," she greeted, halting a few steps away from him.

He smiled at her, as though the new strain on their relationship was nonexistent. Ever since their fight, Sonny had barely stayed at home. He'd even spent the past three nights away, only returning home to pick up a thing or two. So, she hadn't expected to wake up to him in the Jacuzzi.

"Top of the morning to you, beautiful." He outstretched his right hand toward her.

She cast him a wary gaze. It was hard to believe that the same man who'd been avoiding her for three days in a row was acting all friendly. Still, she honored his invitation and bridged the distance between them.

"I'm so sorry, Andrea," he said.

"It's okay—"

"Please," he interrupted. "I shouldn't have acted like that. I overreacted. I was wrong. I admit it. I've hated myself ever since, trying to find a way to make it up to you. I didn't know how to come near you again. I thought you would—"

"Shhh." Andrea crouched beside him, and then she pressed her left index finger to his lips, silencing him. "I should be the one apologizing. I should never have brought that up. It won't happen again, Sonny. I promise. I love you so much and I respect your decision. You are all I need to be happy. Just you."

Sonny planted a soft kiss on her lips. "I love you, too, sexy lady and I wanna make it up to you," he added.

"No, you really don't—"

"Shush your beautiful mouth. I was a jerk and I want to make it up to you."

Sonny held her hand again, and then he gestured for her to get up. She rose to her feet and slipped the thin straps of her gown off her shoulders so the fabric fell to the floor. She stepped out of it and joined Sonny in the Jacuzzi. She sat in front of him with her back to him, and then she leaned against his chest.

He gently moved the Jacuzzi bubbles along her thigh. "I've been thinking and wanted to do something different then the predictable roses or chocolates. So… I decided that I want to give your car a customized detail."

Her back was so flat against his chest that she could feel the rumble of his voice in her own chest. Everything seemed like it was back to normal.

"So I'll need to have it all day." He kissed her neck. "Alright, love?"

"Thank you, husband," Andrea said with a smile.

"Anything for you, babe."

Later that night, a fidgety Olivia sat in the driver's seat of her Camry. She'd parked the car at the entrance of an alleyway. It was just after the laboratory where she worked. She glanced sideways, at the front passenger seat of her car. The envelope containing Sonny's DNA results lay in the seat, waiting to be picked up.

She redirected her attention to the road, hoping Andrea showed up soon. Olivia had arrived at the alleyway no less than five minutes ago. Being out in the streets at night wasn't something she did very often. Sure, she closed late for work, but she always drove home right after. It was impossible not to fidget while she waited.

Andrea's lateness was starting to make her unsettle. What if something had gone wrong? What if Sonny had somehow discovered? If he had, then Andrea would not be the only one in trouble. She would be just as involved. So, she could only hope things hadn't gone out of plan.

The plan had been to meet by ten. It was only five minutes past ten, but Olivia was starting to worry...a lot more than could be considered normal. She didn't know much about Sonny, but she had found out just enough to make her worry. She picked her phone from where she'd mounted it on the dashboard, but she didn't go through with the call.

A car zoomed into view just in time. It slowed to a halt as it neared hers, and then it parked a few steps away. Olivia concluded it was Andrea's car, so when the car honked twice, she knew without a doubt that that was Andrea asking her to come over.

Olivia grabbed the file, hopped out of her car and advanced toward Andrea. From behind, all she could see was Andrea's straight brown hair. She moved quickly, almost breaking into a sprint even though Andrea's car was only a few steps away. She could feel her hair rising as she walked. It caused goose bumps to litter across her skin. She'd say it was the cold evening breeze, but she knew it wasn't just that. That was just her and her baseless fear of the dark. She moved to the front passenger seat of Andrea's car but it was locked. Without a word, she tried the back door and hopped inside.

"Goodness, Andrea!" she exclaimed, heaving a breath. "I was starting to worry."

She shut the door, and then she turned toward Andrea who was still looking straight ahead, as though there were a movie playing out in front of them. Andrea was stiff as a statue. She was apparently lost in thoughts.

"You should be afraid. Very afraid."

Andrea's voice was a tad…weird…? Olivia thought. *Was that the word?* Olivia couldn't place a finger on it. Maybe Andrea still had a cold. That explained why her voice still sounded weird, same way it had when they'd spoken over the phone. Andrea sat still and unmoving. It wasn't hard to realize that she was lost in thoughts about her husband.

"Andrea?" Olivia reached for Andrea's shoulder.

The driver whirled toward her with eyes cold as death. "Yes, darling?"

"Shit!" Olivia muttered.

She was staring right into the eyes of a cold-blooded murderer. The man was calm and unfazed; his skin hiding behind the long sleeves of a turtleneck shirt, while a wig veiled the sides of his face with silky curtains of brown strands of hair.

Her heart slowing to near immobility, Olivia reached sideways, groping for the door handle without breaking her gaze. But the door handle suddenly seemed nonexistent as she felt around with her palm. The man trained his eyes on her. He seemed oblivious to the fact that she was groping for the door. And although she knew a man like him could never be so clueless, she hoped he was truly unmindful to her intention.

She held her breath, preparing herself to leap right out and dash to her door once she found the handle. Sonny's eyes were cold and weakening. They told her she was one easy kill, just like his former boss and the man's wife—the couple that she had discovered he'd murdered in cold blood.

Olivia wished she had gone with her first instinct, which was not to do the investigation. She wished she had told Andrea that she was just being paranoid and to suck up whatever insecurities that she had. No matter how much she wished, her fate seemed sealed. There was no getting out of this predicament.

Sonny grinned. "Hello, doc. You have some information about me, right?" He continued, forcing out a fake laugh while securing his gloves. "Next time, you might wanna…uh…I don't know. Perhaps make sure that you're talking to the right person."

Olivia's heart leaping to her throat, she turned sideways and yanked the door handle. Sonny leapt in the back with the speed of wind. But she never got to see him. He wrapped an arm around his neck, while his other arm found its place behind her head. His grip on her neck tightened, constricting her airways. She choked, her hands darting to her neck in a frantic attempt to pry off the strong arm around it. But the man had her locked in a death grip.

"You know… I will never understand why people can't just mind their own damn business."

Choking sounds escaped her, and the pace of her heartbeat dropped beyond recognition. In that moment, death flashed before her eyes. Olivia knew this was it. She knew there was no escaping him. The snapping sound of her neck amidst the raspy breaths of the murderer was the last thing she'd ever hear.

Chapter Eight

Andrea's whole life just seemed to be falling into place. On one hand, it all seemed too good to be true. But this was Sonny, the super understanding gentleman she'd said 'yes' to. She'd known that the Sonny she knew was still in there somewhere. His offer to add a customized detail to her car was just enough to make her day. So, she totally didn't see it coming when he phoned her an hour ago, saying that he wanted to have a romantic night and discuss the possibility of kids.

Kids! Andrea was still in shock. She hadn't thought this day would ever come, but here it was. Their falling apart sure had a role to play. She grinned as thoughts overwhelmed her. It didn't matter that she was at a drug store and would momentarily become everyone's focus if they caught her grinning like that. There was just no way to keep the emotions bottled up inside of her.

Done shopping, she proceeded out of the store with her shopping bag and headed for the road. If her car were available, she would be home in five minutes, tops. But walking home would make the journey last twice as long. She wasn't complaining though. She needed the walk after all. And besides, she didn't want to walk in on Sonny decorating the house. She doubted he'd like to be interrupted while he was setting the scene. She knew how romantic her husband could get. So, their romantic dinner would only commence after he had decorated the house, the same way he'd done when they made love for the first time, and afterwards on their wedding night.

Andrea wasn't surprised when she walked into a candle-lit room moments later. The scent of lavender greeted her once she stepped into the house. But it was even stronger in the bedroom, dispersed from a humidifier sitting in a corner. Rose petals mapped a path to the bed, with thick candles flanking them on both sides.

Sonny was waiting on the other end of the path, where the trail of roses led. He was as handsome as ever. He watched her with a smile, his hand outstretched toward her in a warm invitation while his soft eyes caressed her from where he stood. A chill ran up her spine at how he still lusted for her after all this time. It was just another part of him that confirmed how amazing he was. She felt that much guiltier about the investigation. After her romantic night, she had planned to call Olivia and tell her to forget it.

She advanced toward him, breaking into a smile. For some reason, it seemed like they were reenacting their wedding day. Maybe it was the radiant smile on his face and the way he outstretched his arm toward her as she advanced toward him. Or perhaps it was the way he was casually clad in a white long sleeve shirt and black pants. He obviously had a thing for white shirts, so that was nothing new. On that night, however, it reminded her of their wedding. He'd been dressed no different.

Once she was close enough to touch him, she reached out her right hand and slipped her hand into his. He closed his fingers over hers, giving her a taste of his warmth. She inhaled deeply, savoring the feel of his fingers on hers.

He yanked her closer, so she fell against his chest. She gasped, her heart lurching. But her startled look transitioned into a smile as she stared into his eyes—an endless sea of caramel. His lips, as inviting as ever, were barely an inch away from hers. They seemed to say 'taste us.'

"Welcome, my lady," Sonny said, his voice almost lost in the soft music playing in the background. "I am your servant and your every wish is my command."

"All of this for me?"

"Who else?" He responded with a sexy, mischievous grin.

He planted a kiss on her forehead. He was in no hurry to pull away. His lips stayed glued to her forehead even after he'd ended the kiss. She wrapped her arms around him and shut her eyes, welcoming the flutter of butterflies triggered by his lips against her skin.

"Wine?" he asked.

She smiled. Sonny needed no further response. She clung to Sonny as he led her to the coffee table where a glass of wine sat amidst two glasses, and after he'd popped the lid, he poured some wine into the glasses.

"Let us toast to our new beginning." Sonny said, picking up the glasses.

"A new beginning?" She questioned.

"Yes. May we always find comfort in one another and share our inner thoughts and desires so that they are fulfilled only by each other." He added, presenting one of the glasses to Andrea.

Andrea smiled as she held the glass. She raised it in midair. "To our new beginning of love, understanding, compassion and compromising."

She clinked her glass against Sonny's, and then she took a sip, her eyes locked on him. The wine traveled down her throat with a sinful sweetness that made her crave some more. Cold and yet fiery, it burned a path down her throat, exposing her to a warmth that hadn't been there before. She emptied her glass in no time. Craving some more, she reached for the bottle, and then she glanced up at Sonny with a sheepish smile. He stood unmoving, his eyes pinning her to the spot. He held his glass against his lower lip, but his wine looked untouched.

She giggled. "Drink up."

Sonny smiled. But it didn't reach his eyes. The look in his eyes had suddenly transitioned from passionate to one she couldn't quite decipher. It was distant and wooden, almost as though the Sonny she knew was gone, instantly replaced by a stranger.

"Sonny?" she called.

A sudden lightheadedness had her swaying on her feet. She shook her head. There was no way this was happening. She had only had one glass. Just one. That wasn't enough to make her tipsy already, or was it?

"Sonny..." she called. Her voice was feeble, but it was the loudest she could reach.

The house spun around her in wild circles, making it seem like there were multiple Sonnys, staring at her with eyes of steel. She could use a chair; she was starting to feel like she was standing in a moving boat. She inched forward on wobbly legs, but her attempt to find support only ended up with her crashing into the floor.

Andrea lay sprawled up on the floor, her blood barely able to fill her veins. She could hear her heartbeat in her throat. It was a sound so loud, it dulled out every other sound, and then it became all she could hear. Her now heavy eyelids fell over her eyes, shutting out the sight of the world. Her vision faded to black, and the last thing she saw were Sonny's shoes.

Chapter Nine

Andrea stirred into consciousness. Her eyes fluttered open, and a pulsating pain in her head shook off the rest of her grogginess as she came to. She moved her hand in an attempt to touch her aching head, but her hands were still. She could barely even move a finger. Her eyes flew open. Round with fear, they settled on Sonny. He was right in front of her, straddling a stool. The sight of her husband should put her at ease, but it didn't.

"Sonny," she called. "What happened?" She tried to think, but her mind was hazy.

"Wake up, sleeping beauty." Sonny said, smiling at her.

"The basement?" She glanced around. "I don't understand… What am I doing here?"

Her voice was softer than it had ever been, as though she'd been screaming for ages and had ended up with a sore throat. But it wasn't her voice that worried her at the moment. She was more confused about how she'd ended up in the basement and why her hands were restrained.

"I don't understand," she said.

She was seated on a chair, her spine straight as a ruler, with her hands behind her back. She attempted to move her hands again, and this time she felt a pressure around her wrists. She didn't want to believe this was what she was thinking, but everything pointed out to the fact that she'd been bound with tape or a rope.

"Sonny?" She cocked an eye at Sonny. "What is going on?"

She tried to stand, but her legs stayed rooted to the spot. She lowered her gaze and found duct tape around her ankles. And then it all came flooding her mind—the memories. *Candles. Soft music. Wine. The wine…*

"You spiked the drink…" she said, shaking her head.

"Only so I could get you here," he said, "right where I wanted you."

He rose from his chair and then he moved behind her. She flinched as he dragged his finger pad across her shoulder blade. But there was no escaping his touch. Her resistance only got her so worked up, making it almost impossible to breathe through the already cloggy air in the basement. She needed the energy.

"Don't touch me," she said, more to herself than to him. "Please."

"Ironic how you were the same bitch craving my touch." He punctuated his words with a chuckle as his raspy voice made Andrea's skin crawl.

He leaned toward her and led his mouth to her left ear, with his hands gripping her shoulders. His breath met her skin, coating it with the venom it spewed out.

"Sonny, please," he said, mimicking her voice, and doing a disgustingly bad job at it. "Please, Sonny, I want you. No rubber. I want to feel your skin. I want to carry your baby. Oh, Sonny…"

"Stop!" Andrea yelled, bursting into tears. "Stop! Please…"

His words had crowded her head with memories that should never have been made. Memories of their naked bodies, sweaty and needy, rocking to the tune of their passion. She lowered her head and shut her eyes, squeezing out her tears.

Sonny grabbed her head and yanked it upward so her neck faced the ceiling. Her neck stretched further than it ever had her whole life. His hands tightened around her head, as though he would crack it open with his bare hands, and then he whispered in an icy voice she could have sworn wasn't his voice.

"The basement. Here is where it all started."

Andrea stayed muted as her neck began to ache even more. She attempted to slowly roll her head around, hoping it would ease the pain. It seemed to only intensify.

"You don't understand, do you?" Sonny continued, shoving off her gesture.

She lowered her head, her tear-smeared chin sinking into her chest. Even when she heard Sonny's receding footsteps, she made no attempt to raise her head. He halted for a moment or two, and then he redirected his steps until he was standing in front of her, with his chair behind him.

"Look at me!" he ordered.

She trembled into submission. Her misty eyes had settled on him. He was now holding a large envelope.

"Atta girl!" He ripped open the envelope, yanked out a sheet of paper and waved it in front of her face. "Didn't think I'd ever find out you were having me investigated, did you?" He huffed out a laugh. "Anyways, here are the DNA results," he said. "I have good news and bad news, Andrea. Which do you want to hear first?"

She glared at him. She didn't know what all of this was about, but this was not her Sonny. This was not the man she'd married. Yes, this had to be one twisted dream or a sick joke. Maybe this was a movie and she'd find a camera. There was just no way this could be reality. So, she tried to suppress her pacing heart in hopes that she would snap out of this nightmare soon.

"Fine, I'll help you decide. I'll give you the bad news first." He said, starting to walk around her in slow, unsettling circles. "The bad news is that your dear Olivia passed away today."

"Oh my God!" Andrea gasped.

Sonny chuckled. "Not to worry. She got you the DNA results before she died. Now, that's the good news. You're probably wondering how I got to know of the DNA. Well, darling, after that incident about you wanting a baby, I knew you had something up your sleeves. So when you received a call from Olivia this morning, I didn't think twice before answering it. And lucky me, I had a cold. It made my voice sound…feminine…just like old times. Having a cold always messes up my voice box implanted in me." He added, touching his throat as a smile tugged at his lips.

"You had a voice box implantation?" Andrea asked.

"News flash!" Sonny grinned. "Oh, and just so you know, darling, your car is still the same. I didn't do any shitty customized detail. That was just me having your car all day so I could go meet Olivia disguised as you."

"Oh my gosh…"

"Yeah, I'm a fucking genius!"

"You sick bastard!"

"Careful…" His voice was laced with venom, conflicting with the smile on his face.

Sonny dropped the DNA results to the floor, and then he overturned the envelope, spilling its contents as well. Although Andrea was trying to restructure her irregular breathing pattern, her curious eyes led to the floor. She grimaced. There were photos all over the floor. Photos of a mixed girl she'd never seen before. The girl was probably in her late teens or early twenties.

She looked up at Sonny, then back at the photos. Why was she staring at a stranger? What did this woman have to do with anything?

Chapter Ten

"Who is she?" she asked.

"Yours truly!" Sonny tossed off the envelope and bowed at her in mock obedience.

"I don't und—"

Sonny scratched his head with his left hand, and then he returned to his chair. He moved it closer to Andrea, and then he straddled it the same way he had before. "This was where it all started, Andrea. The basement." He added, glancing around.

Andrea glanced around as well, but none of his words made any sense to her. At least not yet. They only filled her with terror—an emotion she'd never thought she could ever associate with a man like Sonny.

"The girl in the pictures," he said, his eyes devouring the photos on the floor, "her name was Sandra. She was only eighteen. Her only mistake was that she wanted a life for herself. Her only mistake was that she fucking wanted to find a job, rake some dough and fucking take care of herself. That was all she wanted."

A smile crossed his face. But it held no joy. It was rather wistful, burdened with pain.

"She met this couple," he continued. "They wanted a maid. They took Sandra."

He rose from his seat and squatted beside one of the photos that had overturned when he dropped it to the floor. He turned it around and then he jabbed his left index finger into the forehead of the man in the photo. His wife was beside him, her arm around his neck. They seemed happy. The smiles on their faces were too lively to be forged. Then again, they might have been living a lie, just like Andrea. Sonny put his middle finger to his index finger, mimicking a gun.

"Pow, pow!" He jabbed the woman's head with the theoretical gun. "And...pow!" He chuckled. "You know, I'm wondering how you got a sample of my blood for the DNA."

Andrea looked away, but then she heard a click. She turned toward Sonny, but the colors suddenly drained from her face as she caught herself staring into the barrel of a real gun. He'd apparently flipped it out of the waistband of his pants.

She swallowed a lump in her throat, her eyes trained on the gun. "A stick pen."

"What?"

"I took a sample of your blood with a stick pen. You were asleep."

"Well, Olivia is dead because of your fucked up curiosity. Happy now?"

"You killed her…" Andrea shook her head as pieces fell into place like a puzzle. "You son of a bitch, you fucking killed her!"

"She stepped on my toes." Sonny wiped the left sleeve of his shirt, even though there was apparently no need for that. "And I didn't like it. Just the same way I didn't like it when my pathetic boss and his wife fucking turned me into their sex slave. I was only eighteen. I never deserved a life like that. I was…"

He picked up the photo of the mixed girl, and then he smiled.

"Look how innocent I was, darling…" He presented the photo to her.

"T-that's…you?" Andrea stuttered.

"Yes, darling." He grinned. "I was born a girl. I was a sweet girl who went by the name of Sandra. Spent my past life in Canada. I only moved here after I became Sonny Adams."

Barely tilting her head to the side, Andrea was trying to discern whether or not he was serious. Although the evidence was right in front of her face, it was still too surreal. This couldn't be true.

He hardly gave her a moment to process the news he had just revealed. He went on, "Now you know why I had a voice box implantation. I used to be a girl until I got fucking tired of being locked up in a psycho's basement as a dumb ass sex slave. I needed a way out, so I killed him. I strangled him with the same handcuffs he got for me." He said as he chuckled. "That sick bastard."

"Is this your way of trying to get a divorce?" Andrea asked, confused and not quite sure if she was being sold on what he was saying.

Was this for real? How could someone hide a secret of this caliber? How could someone not only escape murder, but escape their entire life? *How?*

"Believe me, I killed him a thousand times over and over in my head." Sonny continued, ignoring her question. "But his wife...I had no intentions of killing that one. I wanted her. Sex with her was oh so divine. I needed that juicy ass and those big tits. I went to her and asked her to elope with me. But the fool...she told me she was raised to be with a man. Not with me. I decided right then and there that that was the last time any woman would turn me down for that reason."

"You're a hypocrite, Sonny...Sandra or whatever the hell you're pretending to be. You say you killed your boss because you wanted freedom, but you didn't give his wife the freedom to live the way that she wanted to."

He gnashed his teeth and rose to his feet. With his finger on the trigger, he stood directly in front of her.

"Look, I did what I had to do," he replied. "Same way I have to do this..."

Andrea shut her eyes, her heart crumpling into a messy ball. She would plea, but her plea would only energize this man. His other victims—his boss, the man's wife, and now Olivia—had no doubt pleaded. He'd killed them anyway so what was the point? She squeezed her eyes harder as she listened for the ear-splitting sound of a gunshot. But she heard the doorbell instead.

"Fuck!" Sonny yelled. "Fuck! Fuck! Fuck!"

Andrea's eyes narrowed open. Her heart swelled with hope. This was it—her salvation. There was no way Sonny would pull the trigger while someone was just outside. Yes, the man was crazy, but he certainly wasn't stupid.

"You stay right here!" he ordered. "Or I swear I'll kill you..." He paused, and when he spoke again, his voice sent a chill shooting through her. "…slowly…"

Chapter Eleven

Heather. Andrea could hear the woman's voice. Heather was the last person Andrea wanted to see at the moment, but Heather was her salvation. She'd come searching for her dog and Sonny had offered to help. Andrea could hear their footsteps as they walked around the house. She wasn't even the least interested in whatever they were talking about, but when Sonny spoke about a divorce, his words didn't escape her ears.

"I've been living alone for a while now," he said. "Turns out Andrea wasn't the one for me. We're getting a divorce."

"Dear heart!" Heather said. "I didn't know. You guys seemed so perfect together. Are you alright?"

Whatever Sonny said in response, it didn't make it to Andrea's ears. He and Heather had gone out of earshot. Andrea glanced around, frantic for a way out. Her eyes zeroed in on the table a few steps away from her. Careful not to make a sound, she scooted toward the table until her back was barely an inch away from it. Her heart was pacing, her skin covered with a sheen of sweat. If Sonny showed up at that moment, she would be dead in a heartbeat.

"Please hold him for much longer, Heather," she mouthed.

She led her hands to the sharp edge of the table and started to move them up and down, forcing the tape on the edge. Her hands trembled with each move, and her heart thumped as though it would burst out of her chest. But she knew better than to let the emotion overwhelm her.

"Come on! Please!" She whimpered.

She kept moving her hands, pressing them harder into the furniture until she felt the sharp edge biting into the tape. She yanked her wrists apart, ripping off the rest of the tape, and then she bent over to free her legs. The sound of a closing door caused her to halt. But she snapped out of the spell at once and grabbed a baseball bat sitting at the feet of the table. She hastened to the furthest corner of the basement, which turned out to be the darkest corner, and then she crouched, blending into the darkness. The door swung open and Sonny dashed in. Andrea tightened her grip on the bat.

"Shit, shit, shit!" he yelled. "No!"

With the gun in his hand, he hastened to the middle of the room. He glanced around, raking his fingers through his hair, and then he gripped the gun with both hands. He started to circle the room, his eyes sweeping around every corner but Andrea's hideout.

"Come out, come out, wherever you are," he said in a sing-song voice.

Andrea froze as he unknowingly turned toward her. He then whirled around on his heels, so he was standing with his back to her. *Now*! A voice in her head yelled. She leapt out of hiding and struck the back of his head. He screamed like a girl, his gun falling to the floor.

"Turns out it isn't just the cold that messes up your fucking voice box, huh?" Andrea said, delivering another hit.

She raised the bat for a third hit, but he suddenly lunged at her, knocking her into the floor with his momentum. He knocked the bat out of her grip and pinned her to the floor. Her attempts to break free were as feeble as a worm's attempt to escape from a falcon's beak.

"Well, at least nothing messes up the testosterone injections I've been getting, bitch!" he said.

Andrea nodded, or at least she tried to. Sonny countered her nod with a much stronger nod, forcing her head back down. She grunted as pain flashed through her head.

"You are so fine when you're feisty," he stated, watching her with a smirk. "I think I should eat you out and let you cum in my mouth for old time's sake."

"You are a true freak of nature." She hissed.

Ignoring her disgust, he lowered his head toward her chest, but she raised her right knee and slammed it into the crux of his legs, crushing his artificial balls. He yelped, but still found his way to her chest and forced a nipple between his teeth.

Andrea yelled. "Get off me, you bastard!"

"But we're having so much fun, darling. Let's share a final round of passion one last time."

"Sonny?" a voice called.

He noticed it was Heather again. "Shit!" Sonny muttered. "What the fuck is she doing in here?"

For the first time since his captured days, sheer fear had begun to arise within him. He knew that he couldn't allow either woman to escape the basement. There was no question in his mind that he would have to kill Heather, too.

"What's …?" Heather started, but her words died on her lips as Sonny rolled off Andrea and grabbed his gun. She was standing at the first of the stairs leading to the basement, her left hand resting on the wall.

Sonny did a swift roll to his back and squeezed the trigger, hitting Heather with two bullets. Just as Heather's limp body trampled down the stairs, Andrea dashed for the fallen bat, secured it in a tight grip and swung it against Sonny's head as he tried to get off the floor. The impact sent him crashing back down into the floor, where his own blood soon pooled around his head.

The bat slithered out of Andrea's now shaky grip as she watched her husband's body instantly drop just a few steps away from Heather's body. She was hoping he was dead, but she was too afraid to go near him and see. She imagined him waking up and grabbing on to her leg if she tried to run past him. All of the windows to the basement were sealed and the only exit was from upstairs in the home. Andrea knew that she couldn't wait another second.

The house was still as death. Every breath she sucked in was like a shard of glass, puncturing her lungs. On wobbly feet, she finally had gotten the courage to make a move. She quickly headed up the stairs, locked the basement door, and hurried to grab the telephone in the living room. Her shaky hands were barely able to hold the phone.

"911. What's your emergency?"

Epilogue

Andrea was nothing like Sonny. She'd suspected that a strike to the head would not be enough to rid the world of a man like Sonny —or should she say a woman like Sandra? Although she had felt she had been through hell and back, the thought of going back to finish the job with the gun that Sonny had did not cross her mind. She was nothing like him, or perhaps the correct term would be nothing like her.

It was all so confusing. Andrea didn't know how to address her ex-husband anymore. But one thing was sure, Sonny Adams was a monster. Well, at least he got what he deserved. He was finally where he belonged. He'd been transported to Canada to face charges. He might have changed his sex and his name and everything that he was on the outside, but nothing could change the darkness of his heart. Not even death.

Andrea wanted no reminder of the lie she'd lived for the past two years, so she sold Sonny's condo right after their last encounter. She had relocated to another neighborhood, desperate to start life anew, but memories from two months ago would not stop popping into her mind every so often. She had no interest in meeting any neighbors or socializing, period. Thanks to Heather, the decision would be easy.

Heather still remained her least favorite person, yet she wished the woman had not paid for her indiscretions with her limbs. Heather survived the gunshots, but her legs hadn't. Now, she would spend the rest of her life confined to a wheelchair. Andrea had also heard that Heather's husband had another wife with kids outside of her. Perhaps Heather already knew this, but pretended like she was the wife instead. *Poor Heather*, Andrea thought. On the other hand, Heather was just as scheming as Sonny. And people like that always found a way to work things in their favor.

When it came to Andrea's personal life, it was hard for her to even think about the possibility of dating someone. How could she trust anyone to be who they said they were at this point? She would be obsessed with looking at signs of imperfections that may be innocent. She had been with a man for almost two years and had no clue that he was born a she. Sure he was more attentive than most men and had questionable qualities, but doesn't everyone have questionable qualities? The man used condoms, for Christ's sake, knowing that he couldn't get her pregnant!

The deceit was endless. Andrea couldn't decipher what was real or fake about the person Sonny was besides the obvious. Who or what did she fall in love with? Did she fall in love with the delicacies of a woman, or did she fall in love with the act of how she wanted to be treated by a man? *Did this incident somehow make her bi-sexual?* Everything about her life was too much to ponder.

Andrea sighed as she settled into a chair in her kitchen. It was one of four high stool chairs that surrounded a marble island in the center of her large kitchen. Her gaze settled on the center of the island, where she'd placed the newspapers she'd fetched from her mailbox barely an hour ago. She hardly ever had gotten the time to read anything since she was busy with a new workout center that she had invested in about a month ago. She grabbed a sports drink from the refrigerator and slid the papers across the table. She almost knocked over her bottle as her eyes zeroed in on the headline.

International Fugitive on the Run

Without even reading the article, she knew that it was about Sonny. As her eyes searched further down the page, she discovered that her intuition was right. The articles explained how Sandra, who was a female, had undergone surgery and changed her identity to a male named Sonny. The article went into detail about the couple that Sonny admitted killing as well as another woman that may have also been his victim. The article also stated that Sonny may have coerced a guard to aid in his escape by presenting the guard with the opportunity of wealth.

Ultimately, it was the end of the article that made Andrea cringe. Not only had Sonny escaped, but there was some indication that he may have undergone yet another sex change. "Sadly, he could be posing as anyone," quoted a detective.

She turned over to the next page of the continued article and there, Andrea found a mug shot of Sonny. He was staring right at her. She could almost feel his breath on her. She read the unvoiced message in his eyes.

'I will find you.'

About the Author

After entertaining a short modeling/acting career, Nataisha T Hill graduated from MTSU majoring in Mass Communication. After several career changes, she followed her passion to write and didn't look back.

"Thank you for taking the time to read part I of Partially Broken Never Destroyed. I look forward to providing you with future entertainment that you will enjoy."

Feel free to check out the entire series as well as other books also available on Amazon.

Partially Broken Never Destroyed Complete Series

We Were Still Kids

The Doctor's Inn: A Private Practice

A Crime for Two

Alyce Leaves Wonderland

After Dawn Breaks

www.imadethebook.com

Kayla's peace was short lived when Jeremy called her a week later, saying he wanted to make amends and at least be friends. He talked about the things he had done wrong and realizing the error of his ways. He offered to take her out to a friendly dinner so he could explain some of the things that took place. When she asked him why he couldn't just explain himself over the phone, he claimed that it was important to say what he had to say face-to-face. Who was he kidding? She knew what he was up to as always. His little fling didn't turn out as he expected. Although she had absolutely no intentions of getting back with him, she wanted to hear his reason for cheating.

Jeremy and she agreed to meet at one of their favorite restaurants called Parquet's. She figured she would dress sexy in order to rub in all of what he had been missing. She wore a black, off the shoulders, one-piece pantsuit with her leopard pumps that matched her leopard accessories. She still wasn't exactly sure how much information Jeremy had regarding Travis or any of what had went down. Being that it was a small town and one of his basketball friends was at the party with Richard and her, there was no telling what he knew. She arrived at the restaurant and noticed Jeremy was already there. The host directed her to his table and he was sitting there looking quite handsome with his black, short-sleeved polo shirt and dark blue jeans. He got up from the table and greeted her with a hug.

"Damn, girl, you upgraded since you left me, huh?"

"I left you? Is that how it went?" Kayla jokingly replied.

"No, I'm just talking, so what's new in your life? A new man perhaps?"

"Not really, I'm just taking some time to myself. How are you and your new? "

"What makes you think I have a new?"

"Well, there is the fact that I saw you two together one day and then you confirmed it weeks ago."

"Oh, that was nothing."

"So, you ruined something good over a tasteless female."

"It wasn't that, I was just going through some things with my dad and you and I were arguing all the time, I didn't know what to do."

"So, you figured the answer would be to have sex with another woman?"

"That's sort of what I wanted to talk to you about," he sighed and paused. By that time, the server came by to get their drinks.

"Proceed," she said, sounding a bit urgent.

"That girl claiming she is pregnant."

Kayla sat there in dead silence. She could not believe this loser was sitting here telling her he got someone pregnant. What in the hell was he thinking telling her this? As much as she convinced herself that she didn't want him anymore, knowing that he got someone pregnant burned her inside. She could feel the cruelty in her gradually increasing.

"What are you telling me this for, hell, you should've had her here instead of me since you got an extra person to feed."

"Damn, see that's why I wanted to talk to you face-to-face, because I knew if I did it over the phone, you would have just hung up. At least now I know you still care."

"Have you seriously lost your mind? Lose my number and die," she responded as she got up and left from the table not looking back.

"Kayla," he yelled as she was leaving, "KAYLA!"

She jumped in her car, pissed to the limit. She couldn't believe that whorish guy, who called himself a man, would get some random female pregnant. She started feeling even more justified about having sex with Travis. She started to think about how Jeremy would always say he would marry the woman who carried his first child. Then she started to feel nauseated by the thought that he may really love this woman and treat her right. She really couldn't understand why she was so upset. It's not as if this guy treated her like a queen or something, so why was she sweating this issue. Consumed by her thoughts as she pulled into her apartment complex, she didn't notice someone had been following her. She parked her car only to discover to the right side of her was Jeremy's truck. Jeremy had followed her home.

Panic came over her because she didn't know what to do. She pretended to fondle around in her purse until she could think of a good lie. He pretty much knew where the majority of her relatives lived, so she couldn't say it was an aunt or cousin's home. She was busted. She had practically given this mentally deranged man direction to her home. She decided not to worry since 9-1-1 was just a phone call away if he tried something.

"Oh, so you really came up," he said, as Kayla finally got out of her car.

"Yeah, and?"

"Oh, I'm not hating or anything, congratulations."

"Yeah, thanks," she dryly responded.

"It's good to see you're doing good and not being a low-life like all my other ex-girlfriends. Miss independent and I don't need anything from a man," he teased.

"Look, Jeremy, I don't know why you followed me; I said all I had to say at the restaurant."

"That's cool, are you going to invite me in so I can see how you're living?"

"This isn't the time and, plus, I have to be at work here shortly so…"

"How about I call you tonight and we can talk about it," he interrupted.

At this point, she didn't want him in her home, by any means. All she wanted was to see him leave and never return, so she agreed. Much to her surprise, he got in his truck, without any hesitation, and left. She felt relieved and overwhelmed all at once. She was so upset with herself for not going over to her mom's house or stopping by the store or something before going home. She started to wonder if she should buy a bat or something just in case. She had already been thinking of getting a gun, since she was a single female living on her own. Now that Jeremy knew where she stayed, it really wouldn't be such a bad idea.

At work, things weren't going any better. One of the day shift managers had written her up because she got a guest complaint the night before. The complaint claimed she was too slow bringing the food out and after she brought it out, it was cold. She couldn't help one of their lazy night shift cooks didn't feel like re-cleaning the grill. Then, Brandy had called out from work for some reason, so she figured she would have to listen to Rachael simplistic ass all night. One of the night managers informed her that the usual new hire trainer wouldn't be in, so she wanted her to train the new girl, Dana. It was just like them, to write her up and then need a damn favor.

Dana was a medium built chick with long curly hair and smooth brown skin. She had wide hips and a slightly cute face. Her only drawback was her legs were somewhat short, accentuating her too long torso. Kayla discovered that Dana dated one of her cousins back in the day, so the conversation they had while she was training her didn't seem awkward. Kayla told her she should come out with her and Brandy sometimes. Dana promptly accepted her offer. This was cool for Kayla, since her and Dana were single while Brandy was spending more time with her man.

It wasn't too long before Kayla ended her shift when Jeremy called. Just seeing his number on her cell phone made her cringe. She decided not to answer since she seriously didn't feel like dealing with him. Just as she pulled around the corner to her apartment, Jeremy was already sitting in the parking lot. She got out of the car, extremely pissed by his assertiveness. He had a lot of nerve to show up at her home without officially being invited. Why was he harassing her when he had a pregnant girlfriend he needed to attend to? He slowly got out of his car carrying a huge bouquet of red roses in his right hand.

"Hey, beautiful, you have a hard day at work today?"

"Jeremy, I thought I asked you to call me?"

"I did, but you didn't answer."

"I meant before showing up."

"What? Are you unhappy to see me or something, sweetie?"

Kayla just took a deep breath and headed towards the door of her downstairs apartment. Jeremy followed closely behind without saying another word. She opened the door and turned on the chandelier style light in the living room. He then walked ahead of her and voluntarily gave himself a tour.

"Nice place Hi-C," he said, trying to be funny.

"Yeah, thanks." His so-called humor didn't appease her at all.

"Some beautiful roses for the beautiful lady," he said as he handed them to her and sat down on the couch.

"Oh, how sweet, thanks." She was trying not to sound too repugnant, but she really hated his guts.

"You can go ahead and take your shower if you want to, I'll just watch a show or something and if you want me too, I can come in and wash your back like I use to."

She was trying to decide was he joking or had he seriously lost it. Even if she had manure on herself, she would have sat there in it until he left.

"Jeremy, I'm tired as hell so if there is anything that you feel you want to say, feel free to get it off your chest because I'll be going to bed soon."

"Well, you know about what I told you earlier right?" he began.

Kayla nodded her head in agreement as he continued. "You also know that I've wanted a kid for a while and how I feel about having kids and getting married. The problem is, she's having my baby but…I'm in love with you, so what type of solution can I come up with?"

"Therapy?" She couldn't believe she said that aloud.

"Actually, I was thinking of marrying you and later on convincing her to give us custody." He slowly eased a small box out of his pocket, got down on one knee and asked, "Will you marry me?"

It was right there when Kayla really knew that his mind was gone. She guessed the news of that woman being pregnant and whatever he was going through with his father had caused his normal logic to malfunction.

"For some reason, in your brain you've volunteered me to be a step-mom after you've cheated? Are you nuts?"

At that moment, she realized that he was serious. He had really conjured up a mastermind plan to live happily-ever-after with her and his unborn child. She could see the disappointment and anger in his eyes as he rose from the floor and got directly in her face as if he was purposely trying to intimidate her.

"What else do you think you are going to do, get some thug guy who won't do anything for you and cheat on you? All men cheat, Kayla, at least I take care of home."

"No, I'm going to get a man who isn't going to make me feel like I'm less then him and who doesn't disrespect me by calling me inhumane names."

"Grow up, Kayla, and quit crying. That's your problem now, you too proud with your stuck-up ass."

"But you are sitting here trying to marry me, huh?"

"Girl, please, women come a dime a dozen, I can do better than you."

"Good because that puts this ass back on the market."

It was at that point when he realized she no longer belonged to him. She had gotten her own apartment; she was paying her own bills, and didn't need him for anything. Not even the lousy lunch he tried to take her to earlier.

He suddenly grabbed her by her arms and pulled her in towards his body. He forced kisses on her neck while repeating how sorry he was. The more and more she struggled to pull away, the tighter his grip had gotten.

She was beyond terrified and had never been so helpless in her life. It felt as if some hobo had broken into her home and tried to attack her.

"GET OFF OF ME!" she screamed, hoping the next-door neighbors would hear her.

"I'd kill you if I ever even think you've been with somebody else," he raged as he pushed her against the wall.

She continued to scream but it didn't work. She made a swift move and butted him in the face with her forehead as hard as she could. He let go of his grasp and immediately checked his nose. She attempted to run towards the door as quickly as she could while trying to grab her cell phone from her back pocket. As soon as she got her hand on the doorknob, she felt his forceful hands grab her arm as he pulled her back to where he stood and backhand slapped her to the ground. He grabbed the cell phone and threw it up against the wall, breaking it into pieces. He then dragged her by the arms down the hall towards the bedroom while she attempted to kick wildly, frequently throwing him off his balance. He finally managed to get her in the room and then threw her on the bed and sat on her legs while holding her arms to the side.

"Do you realize how much time and money I put into you? For some reason you think another dude is about to reap the benefits. You're mine forever," he vented as he moved closer up on her torso, pinning her arms down with his knees. He began to pull off his shirt. She couldn't even cry. She was in so much shock and disbelief about what was happening in her very own home. He probably had been planning this entire episode since he found out she had an apartment.

She just prayed someone would wake her up from this nightmare. What did she do to deserve such torment? How could a man she has known so long be on top of her about to rape her?

"Kayla, you will never believe what happened," assistant nurse, Rebecca, said as Kayla followed her to a private area. "Destiny is here in the hospital in critical condition."

"What!" Kayla gasped.

"Girl, yes! You know that everyone around here knew she was messing with a married man, so somehow, the wife found out, but that's not the sick part. Supposedly, the wife and the husband ended up tying her up, raping her, and then beating her."

"You're lying!" Kayla exclaimed.

"She is in section B1 of the intensive care unit. You can go see for yourself, and oh, don't tell anyone that I told you," Rebecca said, walking off.

Kayla didn't move. She was trying to process the information in her head. Rebecca had to have been exaggerating, she was known for doing that. Then again, maybe Rebecca was seeing how Kayla would react to the news knowing that Destiny was the one who had gotten her transferred.

Kayla wondered was Rebecca trying to see if she was involved. However, Rebecca couldn't stand Destiny either, since Destiny had slept with her ex-boyfriend, so she knew Rebecca hadn't reformed. She decided to go down to the ICU and see for herself.

<u>Chapter One</u>

"Donna, this wedding reception is nothing short of amazing!" Kelly bragged, one of Donna's coworkers.

"Thank you, girl. You learn to appreciate the finer things in life when your man wants nothing but the best for you. I told you two that this would be a day for everyone to remember."

"Yeah, I must say it's hard to top three fountains of Moët and Gucci watches for the entire wedding party. Now, you just got to make sure he's able to perform since he's almost twenty years your senior," Anthony stated.

"Don't mind him...I mean her," Kelly said as she nudged Anthony in the side.

"Oh, you know I'm not. Anthony probably just wants to get laid by my man because he's run out of men to lay at the office."

"You're lucky it's your wedding day and you look too beautiful for me to roast, bitch."

Beautiful was an understatement for the new Mrs. Donna Carter. Her backless dress accentuated her curvaceous hips as the inseams of her white, sequenced gown pulled closely together to showcase her supple breast. Even Beyoncé herself would have been wowed.

"Excuse me...uh...Kelly, if you don't mind I have to steal my wife for a moment." Troy interrupted, gently waltzing his new bride away from them.

"Did he really just act like I wasn't standing here? See, that's why I don't like his ass."

"I'm sure his ass is the only thing you do like," Kelly said as she snickered.

"No, I am not being funny. He is a total homophobic and that's not cool. Before you know it, he'll make her stop hangin' with us. Yes, you too, bitch, while you're looking all sideways at me."

"Did you forget that we all work at the same place?"

"Duh, he'll make her stop working, genius."

"Donna is not that weak-minded to quit her job."

"With all the money he got he can buy her a new job just like he bought his hair plugs."

"Something is seriously wrong with you," Kelly laughed. "Besides, even if she did quit, she wouldn't quit us."

"Well, either way someone needs to teach him a lesson in manners and acceptance."

"Calm down, Anthony. Don't get your panties in a bunch from over thinking. It could have been a simple oversight. He probably just didn't remember you."

"Bitch, no one forgets the queen. And for your info, I'm not wearing any panties."

"You are so nasty."

"Bitch, you don't know the half of it. Now, let's go get some drinks furbished by Mr. Anti-Homely himself."

Donna followed her husband, noticing that he had a tight squeeze on her hand. Observing that he didn't even acknowledge Anthony, this was probably going to be a brief spill about him being there. Donna didn't care. She knew her friends before she even met Troy, so she refused to let him dictate her relationships.

"What is that thing doing here?" Troy asked as they mingled on the dance floor.

"That is very disrespectful. Anthony is my friend," Donna stated, slightly agitated.

"Whatever it is; I told you that I didn't want it at my wedding."

"This isn't the wedding, it's the reception, and since when did you think that you were going to be able to choose my friends?"

"Thy shall not be disobedient to thine husband."

"Exactly. You are my husband, not my father."

"Perhaps someone should have been your father and taught you right from wrong."

"Are you really doing this on our wedding night?"

"Look, I have a business meeting in about an hour and a half. Finish up with your little friends, so we can still make our flight and I can spoil you in the Caribbean." He said, kissing her on the forehead and walking off to greet his daughter who was waving from the other side of the room to get his attention.

Donna hated when Troy would try to start an argument and then throw something extravagant in her face so that she wouldn't press the issue. Donna had expressed to Troy early on in the relationship that her mother and father both died in a car accident when she was seven. She went from foster home to foster home and the journey was beyond horrifying.

Although Troy sometimes had the jerkiest attitude about things, he treated her like a princess. Money wasn't an object since he was the carpeting tycoon of south Arizona. Besides, she was head-over-hills in love with Troy and would do just about anything to please him.

Troy was older and wasn't as physically active as Donna, but his magic stick still did the trick most of the time. The only drawback was that he couldn't last long unless he took Viagra, which ultimately gave him bad migraines.

Donna sometimes found herself pretending during sex, but Troy was the master at giving oral, which compensated for his stamina shortage. For a middle-aged man he was still very handsome and adventurous. He was actually about a ninety percent upgrade from all the other losers she had dated, so his minor flaws were acceptable.

The only other problem that Donna had was that she didn't like how Troy allowed his daughter to treat her. The nerve of her, Donna thought. Who allows their child to not only be absent from the wedding, but to show up at the reception and not speak? Now that Donna was officially moving into Troy's mansion, Monica had no choice but to abide by her rules whenever she came over to visit. She may not ever acknowledge her as her stepmother, but she sure in the hell was going to respect her as one.

"Monica, I'm glad you decided to come. I see you've changed your mind about your stepmother." Troy said, walking over to embrace his daughter Monica.

"Dad, she's not my mother. She's only about six or seven years older than me. Did you tell mom about the marriage?"

"Age is not defined with love, yet love is graced by infinite passion in youth," he said, totally ignoring her question.

"Yeah...sure, dad. I find it very convenient for a young office assistant to marry a rich mogul who technically could be her dad."

"Outside of love, the benefit of a union should go both ways. You would know that if you didn't have that son-of-a-bitch boyfriend leeching off of you."

"Dad, Eric is trying to open up his own fitness center. How is that leeching?"

"When was the last time he bought you something or paid for a date?"

"Dad, this isn't the time to discuss this. Listen, I need you to wire a thousand dollars in my account."

"Have you spoken to Donna yet?" He asked, totally ignoring her request.

"I was gonna-"

"So you have the guts to ask me for money on my wedding day, but you haven't even spoken to my wife?"

"I'm going now, dad. Could you wire the money now? Please and thank you." She added, walking over towards Donna.

"Hi, Donna. I came to say congratulations and you look nice." Monica stated, in the driest tone.

"Oh, is this your way of trying to act decent or did someone offer you some kind of incentive to talk to me."

"You know...whatever, Donna. You think you know everything, but you're no smarter than I am. We could have practically been in the same school together at some point."

"And it just burns you up that I'm the new apple of your daddy's eyes, doesn't it?

"Be careful what you say to me, Donna. You should always remember that I'll always be his daughter."

"That may be true, but now that we're married, I will always have access to the finances. I suggest you play nice. You wouldn't want the rent on your apartment to accidentally get defaulted."

As Monica walked off with a mean glare on her face, Donna knew that dealing with her was going to be challenging. She was the youngest daughter of her husband's two girls, so he had spoiled her rotten. Perhaps, Troy's missing ex-wife played a role in Monica's lack of respect for her.

Donna found it quite strange that she up and left the kids after the divorce. Although they were grown, it would seem as if she would at least stay in contact with her kids. Almost a year had passed and they heard nothing from her.

According to Troy, their mother did send them gifts with no return address for their birthdays and Christmas. Troy claimed that he loaned their mom some money before she left because she wanted to explore the world with her new friend guy. He also told the girls that their mom still randomly calls him from a private number to check on them. Donna just figured that she had a mental breakdown after the divorce and needed time to find herself. As selfish as it was, their mother being gone was one less person she had to deal with when it came to Troy.

"Drive!" Monica demanded to her boyfriend Eric, who was sitting in the car.

"What's your problem?"

"I literally hate that bitch!"

"Babe, that's his wife. You two are gonna have to find a way to get along."

"Not if I can help it."

"Babe, what are you plotting in that big, pretty head of yours?"

"Don't worry about it, Eric Bernard Ferguson."

"Hey! What did I tell you about calling me by my full name," he quickly said, playfully poking her in the neck.

"Stop!" She complained. "You're so annoying."

"And you're too damn sensitive. You need to just stay out of your dad's and Donna's business."

"Shut up and drive. I'm almost tempted to get rid of you just like I'm going to get rid of dirty Donna."

We Were Still Kids (Sample)

Charlie and Joey stood stiff as they looked at Jodie in awe. Joey was young enough to go for it, but Charlie was skeptical. She couldn't believe that Jodie was falling for it, too.

"He's a liar. How would he know our parents?" Charlie asked.

"Well, he asked me who did we stay with, and when I told him Grandma Rose, he said 'yeah, I know your parents. Y'all are those Johnson kids' and I hadn't told him anything," Jodie explained.

"Well, duh, that's my teacher, so I'm sure it wouldn't be hard for him to remember my last name," Charlie said in a matter-of-fact tone.

"Everybody knows he's just a temporary replacement for Ms. Kindle," teased Jodie.

"So?"

"So…what makes you think you're so special that he learned your last name in one day?"

"At least I don't believe everything I hear. You're more gullible than Joey and he's the youngest."

"And you're just mad he told me about mom and not you because he thinks I'm the pretty one," Jodie snapped back.

"Yeah, pretty ugly," Joey said, playfully pushing Jodie's arm and running towards the porch.

As Jodie ran after him towards the house, Charlie's feelings were hurt. Not because of what Jodie said about their looks; Charlie already knew Jodie was prettier than her. Charlie just didn't think that Mr. Frye would like Jodie more than he liked her.

About an hour or so later grandma had arrived home from work. Charlie was sitting in the front room sulking. She tried to hide her feelings, but she clearly wasn't good at it.

"Pick your face up, girl, before somebody step on it," said Grandma Rose as she walked toward the kitchen.

"Yes, grandma," she softly replied.

"What's the matter with you, Charlie?"

Charlie knew she couldn't hide anything from her grandma, but she didn't want to tell her what was bothering her. Charlie figured she'd whip her butt if she told her grandmother she was sad over something silly such as not being favored by a teacher.

"Everything was going fine until I got to homeroom this morning. We got a new teacher, grandma, and I'm not sure if things will work out," she finally said.

"Oh, it'll be okay, Charlie, I'm sure your teacher will like you just as much as the old teacher did. Now, go wash up for dinner."

"Ok, grandma."

Later that evening, Charlie quietly sat down at the dinner table and kept her mouth full, so she didn't have to do a lot of talking. Grandma told the others Charlie was upset because her old teacher was gone, but Jodie knew better. She knew she had crossed the line. Charlie could tell Jodie felt bad from the way she put her head down every time Charlie looked across the table at her.

After dinner, grandma made them clean up and get ready for bed. Joey had to get his hair brushed every night, so his eczema wouldn't flare up on his scalp. This gave Jodie a little time to talk to Charlie alone. She gave Charlie a push as they hopped in the bed.

"Are u still mad at me?" Jodie asked.

"No, who could stay mad at the prettiest girl in the world."

"Come on, really, Charlie? I didn't mean anything by it, besides; you are my sister, so you look just like me."

"I'm flattered," Charlie said, forging a fake smile.

"Come on, are we cool again, or do I have to call u a pretty toad for the rest of the week?"

They both started to laugh. They laughed so hard that grandma yelled to the back, giving them a warning as they scrambled to get in the bed. Feeling better, Charlie lay down and began to daydream about things she wanted to do on summer break.

"I love you, Charlie poop," Jodie said.

"I love you, too, beautiful toad," responded Charlie with a soft giggle and then they were both fast asleep.

It was finally Friday and the kids were happy that the weekend was approaching. Charlie wasn't as enthusiastic about her new teacher as she was the day before. She couldn't help but think he liked Jodie more than he did her. Jodie wasn't smarter than her or as funny as her. Jodie was only prettier than her and not by much. Charlie knew that teachers had their favorites, but good Lord; Jodie wasn't even in Mr. Frye's class. Maybe he just told Jodie about mom because she was older and assumed Jodie would better understand whatever he told her. On the other hand, Charlie knew it didn't matter because whatever he told Jodie about mom, Jodie would tell her.

Once school was over, Charlie went to meet up with Jodie and Joey outside by the school gymnasium. By the time she rounded the corner, she saw one of Joey's teachers standing with them with a big brown bag in her hand.

"Hey Charlie!" Jodie said as she ran up to her. "Guess what?"

"What?"

"Joey won the brown bag special in his class today!"

"What's the brown bag special?"

"It's fresh tomatoes, bell peppers, onions, carrots, and potatoes from Ms. Noel's garden."

Ms. Noel was the fourth-grade science teacher who had a green thumb. She would sporadically bring vegetables and fruits to school and one lucky kid in her class would win the collection in a drawing. Science was the only class Joey liked, so it was no surprise when he won.

Almost as if he had heard his name, Mr. Frye walked around the corner swinging his keys around his finger. Charlie began to wonder was he following them around the school. Why did he just seem to pop up when they were all together? Mr. Frye's humorous persona soon began to turn into annoyance.

"Hey kids. I found out in the teachers' lounge that little Joey won the brown bag surprise. Congratulations, sport!" He said, rubbing Joey's head.

"Yeah, I'm normally always in trouble, but not this time," Joey gleamed.

"Well, I'll be more than happy to give you guys a lift," offered Mr. Frye.

"No, we're taking the bus," blurted Charlie.

"Charlie, that's not polite. Sure, Mr. Frye, just drop us off where you left us the other day."

"Will do, I just have to stop by my house first."

"Jodie, you know grandma ain't about to play with us being late."

"It's fine, Charlie, trust me."

"No, I'm riding the bus," Charlie argued, storming off from them.

"Charlie, wait." Jodie said, catching up with her. "What's the real problem?"

Charlie couldn't admit that she was upset that her teacher seemed to favor her. It wasn't fair that everyone seemed to like Jodie. Joey had his science teacher, and they all had Grandma. Why couldn't Charlie have one person to herself?

"He's just becoming a weirdo and I don't like it."

"Yeah, but don't you wanna know about momma?"

"Yeah, but-"

"Come on, Charlie poop, I got this. We'll be home before grandma even knows anything."

Charlie was skeptical as she allowed Jodie to grab her hand as she followed her older sister. There was an eerie feeling running through Charlie's veins that she just couldn't shake. It didn't take being a psychic for Charlie to sense something was about to go wrong.

"Brad!" she cried. "Stop it, please."

"Let me go!" He demanded.

"You can't do this! You love me!"

Brad flung open the door and shoved her out. He glared at her, his eyes starting to glaze over as tears fought to break out. "I loved you. But I was a fool. I am done being your play toy. Find another sucker to play your game. Goodbye, Jenna."

He stepped back, away from the threshold, and then he slammed the door, shutting out Jenna's lying face. If he could he would shut out his bitter reality. It was a solemn moment for him. If only he could rewind the instance and not had went for her phone at all.

The living room seemed to spin around him, and he felt himself free-falling. Seven years ago, he had thought he found a rose. How was he to know that the beautiful woman was nothing but a thorn in a roses clothing? She continued to slam her hand against the door as she begged him to talk to her. He stood there on the opposite side, almost tempted to open it but he couldn't. He couldn't allow her to make a mockery of him by trying to justify something that was evident.

She finally gave in by telling him she was going to go to her mom's house. She suggested that he needed some time to cool off and rationalize things. He peeked through the window and watched her slowly walk away while calling someone on her cell phone.

Clutching his head as though he would crack it open, he dropped listlessly on a couch. He still couldn't believe what had transpired in a matter of minutes. He then performed an act he had not attempted since his childhood. It was an act he thought he had outgrown. He wept.